Hello Smokey!

Aimee Aryal

Illustrated by Krystal Higgins

MASCOT BOOKS™

www.mascotbooks.com

It was a beautiful fall day at the
University of Tennessee.

Smokey was on his way to
Neyland Stadium to watch
a football game.

He walked past Ayres Hall.

Two students studying on the lawn
waved, "Hello Smokey!"

Smokey passed by South College – the oldest building on campus.

A professor walked past
and said, "Hello Smokey!"

Smokey walked over to
Hodges Library.

Some friends standing outside said,
"Hello Smokey!"

Smokey stopped to see
the Torchbearer.

A group of UT fans standing nearby
yelled, "Hello Smokey!"

It was almost time for the football game.
As Smokey walked to the stadium,
he passed by some alumni.

The alumni remembered Smokey
from when they went to UT.
They said, "Hello, again, Smokey!"

Finally, Smokey arrived
at Neyland Stadium.

As he ran onto the football field through the Open T, the crowd cheered, "Let's Go Vols!"

Smokey watched the game from
the sidelines and cheered for the team.

The Volunteers scored six points!
The quarterback shouted,
"Touchdown Smokey!"

At half-time the
Pride of the Southland Marching Band
performed on the field.

Smokey and the crowd sang
"Rocky Top."

The Tennessee Volunteers
won the football game!

Smokey gave Coach Fulmer a high-five.
The coach said,
"Great game Smokey!"

After the football game, Smokey
was tired. It had been a long day at
the University of Tennessee.

He walked home and climbed into bed.

"Goodnight Smokey."

For Anna and Maya, and all of
Smokey's little fans. ~ AA

To my family and to Liz and Christine,
for their unwavering support. ~ KH

Special thanks to:

Michael Young

Phillip Fulmer

For information please contact Mascot Books,
P.O. Box 220157, Chantilly, VA 20153-0157.

SMOKEY, UNIVERSITY OF TENNESSEE, T, UT, VOLUNTEERS, VOLS are
registered trademarks of the University of Tennessee and are used under license.

ISBN: 1-932888-09-8

Printed in the United States.

www.mascotbooks.com